# TEAMWORK

# AND

# FRIENDSHIP

THIS IS THE TALE OF THE OTTER BABIES

WHO LIVED IN A TIME OF LORDS AND LADIES

DIFFERENT IN WAYS THEY MADE THE PERFECT PAIR

FROM LOGANS TINY FEET TO EMMAS FUNNY HAIR

THE TOWN FESTIVAL WAS JUST DAYS AWAY

THEY WANTED TO HELP BUT NOT GET IN THE WAY

EMMA SEARCHED FOR DECORATIONS BECAUSE
SHE WAS A VERY GOOD SWIMMER

SHE FOUND A GIANT SHELL THE WHOLE TOWN
COULD SEE GLIMMER

LOGAN WENT TO CATCH FIREFLIES BECAUSE HE
WAS A VERY FAST RUNNER

SO THE FESTIVAL COULD HAVE PRETTY LIGHTS
THAT WOULD MAKE IT FUNNER

BUT THE FOOD WAS STUCK ON A BOAT ALONG THE RIVER

SO EMMA GRABBED A ROPE AND TOLD LOGAN TO COME WITH HER

THEY HAD AN IDEA IT WAS VERY CUNNING

THEY TIED ROPE TO THE BOAT AND LOGAN STARTED RUNNING

EMMA JUMPED IN THE WATER AND BEGAN TO FLOAT

WHILE PADDELING HER FEET SHE PUSHED THE BOAT

THE FOOD MADE IT IN TIME IT WAS A GREAT VICTORY

THE KING AND QUEEN ANNOUNCED THEY WOULD GO DOWN IN HISTORY

THE TWO HAD A BOND THAT COULD NEVER BE BROKEN

AND SO THE FESTIVAL ENDED WITH A TOAST TO EMMA AND LOGAN

THE END

www.ingramcontent.com/pod-product-compliance
Lightning Source LLC
Chambersburg PA
CBHW042135110726
48006CB00003B/887

*9798831548570*